A Purple Heart Christmas

Written by
Taylor Salerno

Illustrated by
Ananta Mohanta

Copyright © 2022 by Taylor Salerno

All rights reserved. This book or parts thereof may not be reproduced in any form, stored in any retrieval system, or transmitted in any form by any means—electronic, mechanical, photocopy, recording, or otherwise—without prior written permission of the publisher/author.

This book is written in honor and remembrance of my Great Grandfather,

Patrick A. Carmody.

He is my hero, a World War II veteran, and the recipient of the Purple Heart medal.

Taylor Salerno

    It was just as I remembered, the red and gold walls were glistening from the light of the chandelier. Dark green pine garland twisted around the gold banisters with red bows. Giant Christmas trees decorated with mini gold disco balls and vintage red silk ornaments were positioned in each corner of the room. The massive foyer felt small with every bump to my shoulder as people raced to the concession stand.

    I pulled my Grandpa Mitch's arm and slid my hand into his rough fingers. I dragged Grandpa to the concession stand as my brother, Dylan, followed behind. While in line, the sound of popping and the smell of butter and salt filled the air.

Just then, I saw the Rockettes® figurine wearing the candy cane striped top with the gold skirt, which has always been my favorite outfit. "Hey Grandpa, may I please get the Rockettes® doll?" I asked.

Grandpa replied, "Of course, you can!"

"Is that for your collection, Taylor?" asked Dylan.

"Yes, I get one every year," I answered with a smile. With my popcorn and my new doll in one hand and Grandpa's hand in the other, we walked away from the concession stand to our seats.

Before the show started, Dylan said, "Hey Grandpa, does Taylor's chain for her Purple Heart pendant look familiar?" He pointed to my necklace with a smirk.

"Why, yes it does. Is that the one I got you a few years ago?" asked Grandpa Mitch with a smile.

"Yes, it is. Her other chain broke, so I gave her mine," replied Dylan.

"Nice, how long ago did you get the Purple Heart pendant, Taylor?" asked Grandpa Mitch.

"I have had my Purple Heart pendant since my tenth birthday," I answered proudly.

Dylan interrupted, "And she wears it everyday."

    Then, with a slight smile, I picked up my Purple Heart pendant. I remembered the story of Great Grandpa Pat, who was awarded the Purple Heart Medal in World War II. I wear it to honor him and what he fought for, even though I never met him. Suddenly, the lights dimmed, and the audience went quiet.

Immediately, I knew the show was coming to an end because a red velvet hat with a white pom-pom was coming onto the stage in his sleigh. Attached to the sleigh, the reindeer Rockettes® wore red velvet blazers with gold glitter collars glistening in the spotlight. "Can everyone make a Christmas Eve wish?" asked Santa. I looked down at my Purple Heart pendant and wished that my Great Grandpa Pat could be here to spend Christmas with me.

As we left Radio City Music Hall®, Dylan asked me, "So Taylor, what did you wish for?"

I replied, "I can't tell you or it won't come true, Dylan." Dylan responded with a shoulder shrug.

When we arrived back at the hotel, Mom and Dad had dinner set up on the rooftop. It overlooked the Rockefeller Center Christmas Tree® with millions of lights and ornaments. I could barely see the actual tree. Best of all, I could see the 9-foot-tall star made of Swarovski® crystals glowing on top. I could smell the cinnamon coming from the Christmas cookies at the dessert table and the peppermint from the candy canes in the hot cocoa. Finally, the amazing meal my mom had made with turkey, stuffing, and mashed potatoes was ready.

We took our seats and began passing around the food. Just as Grandpa Mitch handed me the turkey, Dylan screamed, "EVERYONE MOVE!"

CRASH!

BOOM!

Suddenly, all I saw were a bunch of antlers coming towards me...

Santa had crashed into the dinner table. My arm was injured during the crash.

Santa quickly approached me. He looked down at me and I noticed my Purple Heart pendant necklace was glowing. With Santa and his Christmas magic, he granted me the Christmas wish that I made earlier that day at the Rockettes® show.

Just then, I heard propellers from an Army helicopter. Next, I saw a spotlight shining down onto the rooftop. When the helicopter got above the rooftop, a ladder dropped. Suddendly, I noticed black Army boots making their way down the ladder. The Army man jumped from the ladder onto the rooftop.

    As he turned around, I began to light up with joy. I immediately recognized the man. He looked just how I imagined him. My wish had come true, it was my Great Grandpa Pat.

With my necklace still glowing, he came to my aid carrying a tactical first aid kit. Stunned, I stuttered, "Great Grandpa Pat?"

"Hi Taylor, I will have you feeling better in no time. Are you hurt anyplace else?" he said with a warm smile.

"No, just my arm, Great Grandpa Pat," I explained. He cleaned the wound caused by the reindeer's antler and applied iodine to the wound. He covered it with gauze and wrapped it with an elastic bandage. I watched his every move, still amazed that it was really him.

Great Grandpa Pat noticed my Purple Heart pendant was glowing. He reached forward and held it in his hand as he asked, "What is this?"

"Oh," I said with my cheeks turning red, "that is my mini Purple Heart pendant that I wear to honor you."

Stunned, he responded," Why..uh thank you.. um that means a lot." He gently placed the glowing Purple Heart pendant on my neck and smiled.

When I finally looked around, I noticed everyone else was astonished.

    While I was feeling better, Santa's sleigh was still broken. As a result, I had to come up with a way to fix it. Then, I looked up and saw that the helicopter had not left yet. I had an idea! I used the ladder and extra parts of the broken dinner table to attach the sleigh to the helicopter. Next, I asked the Army pilot to fly Santa around until the elves could get there to help with the sleigh.

Now that Santa's sleigh was fixed, we needed dinner. Although Santa's sleigh had crashed into the table and most of the food was ruined, I had a solution. I ordered two large pepperoni pizzas to be delivered to the hotel. Great Grandpa Pat and I went down to the hotel courtyard to pick them up.

When we got back up to the roof, Grandpa Mitch and Dad had cleaned up and rearranged the tables. Dad placed an extra chair next to mine for Great Grandpa Pat. We all sat down in our seats and ate our Christmas Eve dinner. Great Grandpa Pat came over to me and placed his hand on my shoulder. I turned to him. I looked up at him and smiled, "I love you Great Grandpa."

He smiled back at me lovingly, and said, "This is the best Christmas ever. I love you, Taylor."

As I looked around the dinner table, I realized that my Christmas wish had come true. The night clearly did not go as planned, but it was magical nonetheless.

Patrick A. Carmody

Patrick A. Carmody was born on October, 5, 1923 in Manhattan, New York. In 1939, he joined the National Guard on 168th Street in the Bronx. By 1940, he was part of the United States Army, 27th Division in New York State, which was sent to Fort McClellan, Alabama. While in Alabama he married the love of his life, Ruth Magnotto on November 12, 1940. Soon after, the Japanese attacked Pearl Harbor on December 7, 1941. Within two weeks of the attack, he was sent to California to guard aircraft carriers and the beaches.

Then, he was sent overseas. He fought in the Gilbert Islands, Marshall Islands, Mariana Islands, and Okinawa. During combat on February 26, 1944, he was in an incomplete dugout shelter when a member of his battalion jumped out. He and his Chief grabbed him, pulled him down, and jumped on top of him. At that time, a grenade hit and his back was filled with hundreds of pieces of shrapnel. He was in the hospital overnight and returned to battle. It would be over thirty years until the last piece of shrapnel was removed from his back.

Patrick and Ruth Carmody

He went on to fight in combat until the war ended. He received an honorable discharge on September 21, 1945 as a Sergeant, in Company A, 152nd Engineer Combat Battalion. He was later awarded the Purple Heart Medal.

After the Army, he returned to his love, Ruth, affectionately known as Ruthie. They were happily married and raised two girls, Lynn and Patricia, in the Bronx. Pat loved reading, listening to Big Band music, football, and most of all his family.

He passed away on December 19, 1994 surrounded by his loved ones. At the time of his death, he had five grandchildren: Michael, Christopher, Joanna, Lisa, and Sara. Since his passing, his family has grown to include Michael Patrick, Dylan, Taylor, Bianca, Kaleb, and Scarlet. His legacy lives on through his family and all the wonderful memories of him.

According to the United States Department of Veteran Affairs, the Purple Heart Medal is both the nation's oldest and one of the most recognized and respected medals that is awarded to members of the U.S. armed forces. In 1782, General George Washington introduced the "Badge of Military Merit" which is now known as the Purple Heart. On the anniversary of President George Washington's 200th birthday, February 22, 1932, the Purple Heart Medal was reintroduced. The back of the medal features the words, "For Military Merit," engraved. The front of the medal features George Washington's profile placed on a purple heart with a gold border.

When the Purple Heart medal was reintroduced, it was awarded to the U.S. Army. It was awarded to men and women in the U.S. Army that were wounded or killed in action with the enemy. The wounds required treatment by a medical officer, and must have been considered a deserving action of the award which was faithful to the cause. In 1942, President Franklin D. Roosevelt authorized the Purple Heart to be given to all military members. In 1984, President Ronald Reagan authorized the medal could be given in the event of terrorist attacks or peace keeping missions

For more information visit the website below:
https://www.va.gov/opa/publications/celebrate/purple-heart.pdf

"Celebrating America's Freedoms: History of the Purple Heart." www.va.gov, U.S. Department of Veteran Affairs, 20 July 2015, https://www.va.gov/opa/publications/celebrate/purple-heart.pdf.

About the Author

Taylor Salerno is a 12 year old girl who loves Christmas, all things New York, and wishes she could meet her Great Grandpa Pat. She originally wrote this story for her English class. Then, she realized how much she loved the story and decided to make it into a children's book. Taylor currently lives in a Purple Heart City. She was born in New York City. She frequently returns to visit her family  and favorite places. A family holiday tradition of Taylor's is attending the Christmas Spectacular Starring the Radio City Rockettes ® at Radio City Music Hall ®. This has served as inspiration for this story. She hopes that by reading this book, it will encourage more people to learn about the Purple Heart and appreciate the sacrifices of our Veterans.

Made in the USA
Middletown, DE
23 October 2022